Keep in mind that you

are making memories.

Consider that something you take for granted today may be the one thing you might pine for someday, and there might not be any more of it left, but you'll remember its sweetness.

Remember the curve of the sun in
your bedroom window late in the
day, the way your little brother's hair
smelled after his bath, and the sound
of your mother and father talking
in the kitchen.

Make sure you notice if the trees meet in an arch over your street, or if there's a certain sound that you hear at a particular time every day.

*Take note of those people who are
so familiar to you, and consider
memorizing them for a time
when they are gone.*

And know that if anyone ever says to you, "What will you always remember about this place?"

you will know just exactly which

story it is that you would tell them.

OUR

HO

Pictures by

BRIAN SELZNICK

10th ANNIVERSARY EDITION

USE

BY PAM CONRAD

SCHOLASTIC PRESS · NEW YORK

LIBRARY OF CONGRESS CATALOGING-IN-PUBLICATION DATA

Conrad, Pam.

Our house / by Pam Conrad; pictures by Brian Selznick.

— [Special 10th anniversary ed.]   p. cm.

Summary: Six stories, one from each decade from the 1940s to the 1990s, about children growing up in Levittown, New York.

ISBN 0-439-74508-X

1. Children's stories, American. 2. Levittown (N.Y.)—History—20th century—Juvenile fiction. [1. Levittown (N.Y.)—History—20th century—Fiction. 2. Short stories.]

I. Selznick, Brian, ill. II. Title.

PZ7.C76476Ou 2005   [Fic]—dc22   2004065082

10 9 8 7 6 5 4 3 2 1   05 06 07 08 09

Printed in the United States of America   23

First edition, December 2005

The display type was set in Neutraface.

The text type was set in 13-point Fairfield Medium.

Book design by Brian Selznick and David Saylor

The artwork was created in pencil on paper.

In memory of

RAY MONTELLA

P. C.

———

for

PAM CONRAD

B. S.

FIRST,

THE POTATO FIELDS

An introduction

There was once a time when all you could see from this very spot were acres and acres of potato fields. There was a family who worked this potato farm, who turned the soil, planted the potatoes, and prayed for rain. Each night they'd come home to their farmhouse at sunset and kick the dust off their shoes—Long Island dust—dust as smooth as flour. Any kid who's ever lived here will tell you that this Long Island dust can cover your hands and arms, bury itself in your shoes, get in your hair and, still, you never feel dirty. It's a dirt that smells clean and fresh, and sometimes forms into little hard balls that burst into clouds if you pinch them between your fingers.

They used to call this farmland Island Trees. Island Trees, imagine that. Now who names places, anyway? Some politician who was trying to make it sound like something it's not? This piece of land is no island. The ocean is ten miles south, and the Long Island Sound is even farther in the opposite direction.

The truth is those farm kids who used to live here—well, if they had stood on the roof of their barn and looked off, they would have seen a cluster of trees down around where Jerusalem Avenue and Bethpage Road cross today: an island of trees. So that's how *that* happened.

The potato farm that was here grew potatoes all through the Second World War, and at the end of the war, when the soldiers returned from their battles, there a hunger to make families, as though the earth was stocking up again after a terrible loss. People needed houses. They needed a place to put their furniture and park their cars, and a place to raise children who might like to play in dirt.

There must have been a greater need for houses than for potato fields, because when a man named Levitt came along with a plan to build, it was as though that farmland had been sleeping and just waiting for him. The farmer was paid a handsome sum for his fields, and it's thought he moved out east farther to buy himself a bigger farm. Then in a short amount of time, where there had once been a potato farm, there were now houses, row after row of houses.

A lot of people made fun of those houses, laughing at how fast they were built, like Fords on an assembly line. People who saw what happened say it went something like this. First, a brigade of heavy trucks would come tearing down the smooth new roads that had been laid out. Where each house was destined to be, the trucks would dump identical piles of pipes, wood, bricks, copper tubes, and shingles. Bam, bam, bam, just like that, at each site.

Then a battalion of huge machines came through and tore up the land at each site. Each future house was marked with a neat 25- by 32-foot ditch. After that came the legions of cement trucks that would pour a foundation in thirteen minutes flat. And as soon as the cement was dry, gangs of men were there, three or four to a house, and they worked like ants, laying the brickwork, raising the frame, the rafters, hammering shingles, painting the walls. Each small crew of men specialized in a job, and as soon as they were done they moved on rapidly to the next house. They said that in this way, Mr. Levitt was able to finish a house every fifteen minutes.

People swore these houses weren't any good because they were built too fast and they didn't even have basements. But that didn't stop families from lining up, young soldiers freed from the war, with their young wives and babies, and they stood in long lines and waited for hours to sign their names to contracts in order to buy one of those houses. Mr. Levitt sold them for $6990, with a four percent GI loan.

Never had life seemed so good, and never had Island Trees been so full of life. But that first year, 1947, it was as though all the prayers ever offered up for a farmer's rain had suddenly been answered all at once. The skies opened on the new little houses that stood in curved and irregular patterns. The wide Long Island sky swept over them. It rained so hard and so long that the young couples had to lay wooden planks in the mud so they could get to their front doors.

But everyone was very excited. Everyone knew this was the start of a good and new life. They made plans to plant gardens and to seed lawns, plans to build bedrooms in the upstairs attics, plans to build carports and put up swings, plans for barbecues and parades, for schools and for a fire department. And the old name Island Trees had gone the way of the potatoes. The builder, proud and possessive of all he had done, named the town after himself.

And this—all that you can see before you now—is Levittown. Years have passed. Mr. Levitt has died, and his town has gone through many seasons and countless changes. The houses have proven themselves durable and steadfast.

What wonderful tales their silent walls must hold!

Luckily we have the children who grew up in Levittown, hundreds and hundreds of children. Some are still young and are building their memories day by day, and some have grown up and moved away. But all children, young and old, have stories to tell, stories like these—stories of Levittown.

BOY FOSSIL

1948

My name is TeeWee Tator, and yesterday afternoon my father put my feet in cement and memorialized me for all time. He smoothed out a level stretch of wet cement so that my mother can have a nice patio out the back door, and when the job was done, but the cement still soft, my father lifted me by the armpits and held me out over the cement so that just the soles of my shoes pressed in. It was the exact amount of weight to form a good print, and when he went inside to wash up,

I took a twig and wrote beneath my prints TEEWEE T.
I should also tell you that it's 1948, summer of,
and as long as these streets and roads hold up, no
one will ever forget me.

The thing that I'll never forget about living in
Levittown was the night my parents had the
wrestling party and I made an unplanned, and surprise, entrance. But to make sure you understand
exactly what happened, I have to tell you about
our house and how everything is situated in it.

First, when you come in the front door you're
standing in the living room. Off to the right is the
kitchen with another door that leads out into the
backyard. Come back into the living room, and if
you walk along the wall of bookshelves where we
eventually put the television set (which was really
the cause of all the commotion), you come to a
hall. On the left is my mother and father's bedroom, and on the right is my bedroom, where I
was supposed to be that night.

The neat thing, though, which I've saved for

last, is the staircase that goes up right in front of you when you step in the front door. Some people around here don't have a full staircase. Instead they have a handle on the ceiling that they pull, and a sort of collapsible stairway comes down. My mother had insisted on having a regular staircase built, which my father thought was really dumb because it takes up so much room and it really doesn't go anywhere except to an unfinished attic. Dad calls it her "stairway to the stars." Company comes and when they come in the door, the first thing he says is, "Here it is folks, Dolores's stairway to the stars." My mother sort of ignores him and takes everyone's coats to lay on her bed, telling them it's her stairway to the laundry, because that's where she hangs the wet laundry when it's raining out.

It used to be I was only allowed up in the attic when a grownup was with me. Now I'm not allowed up there at all till further notice. Too bad, because it's a great place. It's the inside of the roof with all the bare rafters and beams showing, and you can see how high up the peak goes and the brick chimney that comes up out of the furnace. Down the center of the attic room, there's a floor laid for a walkway where you're supposed to stay. And if you do have to walk out in either direction over the rooms below, you're supposed to stay on the beams, which is not a problem. I guess. If you're a tightrope performer.

My mother gets to go up there anytime she does laundry and can't hang it outside. Each house here in Levittown was originally supplied with one umbrella laundry pole, much nicer, my mother says, than those straight lines in the city that go from windows to telephone poles. And it's what my mother usually uses unless it's a weekend, when you're not allowed to hang laundry out, or unless it's raining. I remember one particular time when it was pouring outside and I followed her up. We were both very quiet, and the sound of the rain on the roof was like nothing I'd ever heard before. It was so quiet and so noisy all at the same time, as though it were just filling our heads with softness.

So as I was telling you before, downstairs there's a television set on the living room wall, built right into the bookcase. Now this may not seem like a big deal to you, but so far we're the only ones on the block with a television set. And the reason we have one is that my mother's brother, Uncle Richie, works for Admiral. He's a scientist, but no one in the family really understands what it is he does. One afternoon I got home from school and there was Uncle Richie unpacking a crate and wiring this box contraption up to the wall.

"Do you know why they call it a television set, TeeWee?" he asked. (Scientists think this way. You get used to it.)

"After the man who invented it?" I asked, peering over his shoulder as he got the box to hum and crackle.

"Tele. Vision," he answered, as though that

would explain everything. "Tele. Vision."

I waited.

"*Tele* originally has its roots in old language meaning things like danger, snare, or trap. Sometimes it refers to spiderwebs."

I kept my eye on the small screen. My one hand could have covered it completely. "Spiderwebs?"

"And *vision*, of course, refers to our sight. So, do you think it could mean an appliance that is meant to trap our sight?"

I shrugged, imagining that once he got it working, I would not be able to look away, that my eyes would be glued to it, eternally and hopelessly glued to the screen. I narrowed my eyes.

"More than likely it refers to the scientific term connected to special appliances or methods that operate over long distances. The first set was actually called a *televista* by the man who invented it. And what it does is, it electronically transmits through the air an image of a moving scene."

"A moving scene?" I asked. "Like what?"

.   .   .

"Like what" turned out to be wrestling matches. Every Friday night this wonder of modern science drew neighbors from up and down the block to our house to watch wrestling. My mother would put out soda, pretzels, and Wise potato chips for during the match, while they all sat on kitchen chairs pulled up to the television set, and then when the matches were over, they'd all have coffee and her special tomato cake, which she'd put out in the kitchen.

This one particular night that I told you I'd never forget, the Thomases were coming for wrestling and also the Trezzas from next door. Andy Trezza's my best friend. He's a year younger than I am, but he's big for his age and I'm small for mine, so sometimes people think it's the other way around. Well, this one night my mother had agreed to let Andy come with his parents and then he could sleep over and have breakfast with us the next morning. We were really excited. All we were going to do was hang out in my room and maybe put something together with both our Erector sets, and then maybe shine the flashlight back over to dumb Herbie's bedroom, and I swear that's all I was thinking of doing, but then it started to rain. The Trezzas and the Thomases were coming in the front door, stomping their feet and laughing, and I could hear the wind and the rain hitting the windows. I could imagine the sounds in the attic.

Andy came back to my room and as soon as I saw him I pulled him in and closed the door behind him. "Shhh!" I warned. "Don't say a word. I have a plan. Got your flashlight?"

He pulled it from his back pocket and grinned. Good ole Andy, ready for anything.

Now to this day I don't know how we pulled this off with no one seeing us. The best I can figure is that my mother must have been in her bedroom with the coats and maybe the ladies, and my father was probably showing off the window shelf he had added in the kitchen. Andy and I just slipped by everyone and silently padded up the stairs to the attic. Not a soul saw us. They must have thought we were in my bedroom. And closing the attic door behind us at the top of the stairs, we crouched down on the walkway in the cold with just the flashlight for light.

We sat with the light off for a long time, just listening to the rain and also to our parents downstairs laughing and talking. Their voices carried easily to us, and we could hear them cheering the wrestlers on, and Mrs. Trezza would start yelling, "Kill Gorgeous George!" and we thought we'd choke to death trying not to laugh. But the loudest thing was the rain, pelting the roof, and the wind, pounding at the shingles just an arm's reach away from us. We felt like spies. Like fugitives. Like escapees from a warlord. A prison. A private school. The possibilities were endless, and we began to spin our web of games there in the dark.

Andy was the first to go out on the beams. He crawled along, with the flashlight sticking out of his pocket. It sent an eerie light into the rafters. He was an evil mountain climber heading out over

Dead Man's Pass, and there was a twenty-mile drop on either side of him. I started out after him to shoot him down and get the gold, but he had a head start, and I couldn't waste my time crawling so I started to leap from beam to beam. So then *he* started to leap from beam to beam. So you see, it was both of us. Anyway, I doubled back to get my long-range rifle and next thing I knew I was standing in my mother's cake downstairs.

Well, not exactly the first thing. First it was this rattlesnake that sprang up in front of me, and I lost my balance, and both feet seemed to go in slow motion, right exactly between the beams. I felt my weight crunch through, and then I was hanging by my shoulders. My legs were gone, but I could see Andy's face, openmouthed, dumb as you please, and then the next thing I was hanging from the kitchen ceiling by my fingers and shreds of my shirt, looking at six adults peering at me from the doorway to the kitchen with the same dumb looks on their faces. That was when I let go and landed in the cake. The table collapsed, and my father was right there. He stood me up so quick and started to pat me and check me over, looking like he was real scared, and I think he would have eventually gotten to real mad except that everyone started to laugh. My mother was laughing so hard, tears were rolling down her cheeks. And when Andy's mother called him and he stuck his head through the ceiling and got yelled at, my mother got worse and they had to take her in the living room and sit her down.

Later they said it was something like nervous hystericals she had, but every time she thought of that night after that, like when they had to repair the ceiling, or she was bringing that tomato cake to some party, she would start all over, the laughing perking from inside her like coffee in the hot percolator.

It's good to have a mother with a sense of humor and love of good memories. That's why I knew she wouldn't be mad when I wrote TEEWEE T under my cement prints. Some things you just never want to forget.

NIGHT
PHOTOGRAPH

1951

My name is Patricia Marjorie Allen and I moved to Levittown when I was seven years old. I'm just about eleven now, so it's been four years altogether that my family has lived in this house. On one side we've got the Abrams family. On the other side our neighbors are the Atchinsons. We're lined up in alphabetical order, and it isn't till you get to the next block that you get into any B's. It has something to do with the way these houses around here were sold.

I'm sure everyone who lives here would tell you something different about Levittown. If you asked my mother what was the best part of living here, she'd probably tell you it's not having to drag the stroller up and down three flights of steps every day like she did when we lived in the apartment in Brooklyn that we shared with my grandparents.

My father might say it's the Long Island Railroad that he takes to work. The man reads four books a week, and swears by the railroad, saying he gets a seat every day and it beats the old subway where he had to stand all the way to midtown.

But if you ask me what my favorite part of living in Levittown has been, I'd have to say without a doubt, without even thinking about it, that it was the time Mr. Leo Choplin came to take the "night photograph" of Levittown from the water tower and lit the streets with flashes from fifteen hundred flashbulbs.

•   •   •

One thing you should know about me is I've always had an interest in photography, and when I grow up I want to be a star reporter for a newspaper in a big city. I read *Superman* comics all the time and I guess you could say Lois Lane is my hero. But I wouldn't want to be just an ordinary reporter. I'd be the kind who gets right in there and takes photographs, too.

I know a lot about photography because of my father. He works for an accounting firm in New York City, and he says he does that to get medical coverage and a pension, but what he *really* does is photography. Every weekend, either on Saturday or Sunday (my mother puts her foot down about him doing more than that), he goes to weddings and takes pictures of brides and grooms and all the gowns and flowers and relatives. And then he develops the prints.

Usually he develops at night and he makes sure everybody goes to the bathroom before he starts. "Bathroom's closing up for the night," he announces after our baths, and everybody finishes up. He's serious about it. One night my brother had to go once my father had started, and my mother made him go next door to the Abramses' house. The worst was when my mother's Bendix washing machine overflowed all over the kitchen floor because she forgot to put the hose in the sink, and still my father wouldn't stop what he was doing to come out and help.

I understand why it has to be this way, because sometimes, if I don't have school the next day, my father lets me help him. He has special drapes he hangs over the small bathroom window and even over the door. Because if even the tiniest bit of light gets in, it can ruin everything. Then he sets up the enlarger and the trays. Everything has to be just right. He pours weird-smelling chemicals into the trays and he lets me be in charge of the hose that runs into the tray in the tub. I make sure it keeps overflowing and rinsing the photographs.

When everything is set up, he turns off the regular light and turns on a red light that makes everything eerie. Then, working in a red glow, he puts the negative in the enlarger, and focuses it. Next he gets the paper out, exposes a sheet to the focused light, and, finally, slips the sheet of paper into the first chemical. He swishes it around, keeps the paper swaying, and it doesn't take long—maybe seconds—before a bride appears.

I used to show my brother, Douglas, how to do this. We'd draw pictures of brides and parties on pads of white paper and then in the bathroom, with the light out, but the sun shining a bit through the shuttered window, we'd soak the drawings in the sink and the tub and then finally line them up to dry on the floor.

My father knew how much I loved this and for my eleventh birthday he gave me my very own Kodak Hawkeye camera. Then I had to figure out what to take pictures of. My speciality became surprise pictures: my mother with her hair in pin curls, my father in his boxer shorts getting a mid-night snack, or Douglas the time he fell asleep in the car and they left him there awhile. Some of these pictures came out dark, mostly shadows.

My dad told me how you need to use flash-bulbs for nighttime pictures, so he encouraged me to take most of my pictures outside when the sun was shining. That's why I knew if *I* wanted to take a picture of Levittown, I'd have to do it in broad daylight, but it was Mr. Leo Choplin who gave me the idea about the water tower.

Word got out the day before the picture-taking. This was the first I heard that a "night photo-graph" was going to be taken from the water tower. The tower's just a couple of blocks from here. We can see it from our back steps, so I was ready early that morning. I got there just as the men were arriving in their trucks. I took a picture of them unloading. They unloaded boxes and boxes of bulbs and equipment, and I took a pic-ture of the piles of boxes, too. One man seemed to be in charge of everything. The others asked him questions and called him Leo. He was a big man and while he directed the others to carry up the cables and boxes of flashbulbs, he insisted on carrying the cameras himself. As he stood at the bottom of the ladder to the water tower, one foot on a rung, one big camera under his arm, I took a picture of him. He didn't say anything just then, but he smiled at me.

It took them all day to get things ready—aiming the three cameras, attaching the flash cubes in their big reflectors, and all over the neighborhood men with walkie-talkies were walking up and down blocks that were within sight of the tower. When I went home for lunch, excited to tell my mother what was going on, one man tramped right through our backyard with the walkie-talkie pressed to his mouth. "How's this?" he was saying. "Can you get this in over here? I'd say you've got a good shot from this angle."

My mom peered out the kitchen window at him. "I hope he doesn't walk on the new seed your father just put down." And then, to my shock, she added, "And don't get any ideas about that water tower, Patty." She didn't take her eyes off the man walking through her pansies. I didn't take my eyes off the last bit of my cream cheese and jelly and banana sandwich, as though going up in the water tower had never occurred to me.

"What's he doing now?" I asked to distract her.

"Going over to the Abramses'. Right through the forsythia bush."

I gulped my glass of milk and bolted for the door. "Gotta go! See you later!" I called, and she called something back, but I was out the door and long gone, and glad she had no walkie-talkie.

In the early afternoon light, the water tower loomed above me. Off to the side, the workmen were gathered around the two trucks, eating lunch. They sat in the shade of the open backs of the trucks and under the few trees at the curb. They ate quietly, laughing and talking. They had left the expanded ladder to the water tower down, and it clanked softly when I put my weight on it. I froze, but their voices didn't change. I slipped my Hawkeye camera strap over my wrist and pushed it as far as it would go up my arm. Hand over hand, foot over foot, I climbed the ladder up the water tower. It was not tilted like a ladder leaning on the side of a house, but it went straight up like a tightrope walker's. I didn't dare look down. Up and up, I thought I'd never get to the top, and my hands were shaky by the time I did.

I held on tight with one hand and shook my arm to bring my camera down to my wrist. I eased it into my hand and looped my elbow through the hard metal ladder to hold me. I was breathing hard and beginning to get an awful feeling, as though I were part of some Our Gang comedy skit, like I was Alfalfa or Spanky, and any minute I'd be yelling for help. But I held on.

I put the camera up to my eye and faced in the direction of my own house. I prayed my mother wasn't looking out at that moment. There it was, like a little dollhouse, with its brick chimney and yellow siding, and the redbrick patio out back. I could see the pink curtains to my bedroom, parted in an upside-down V. How many nights had I

33

stared up at the water tower from that window?

I held my breath. I held as steady as I could and slowly pressed the shutter. Click. Then I looked for Gayle's house. She was my best friend, but she was in Montauk for the summer. Click. I snapped that one, too. I looked around. There was my school. Click. And the pool. Click. And I was sure I could see Hicksville and Bethpage from there, but my camera suddenly locked. I was out of film.

I had another roll in my pocket. Clinging to the ladder with one hand and reaching deep into my pocket, I forgot to loop the camera around my wrist. It tilted off the rung of the ladder. I reached for it, but my reaching pushed it farther. It teetered in the air, an inch from my fingers. Then it went plunging down toward the grass below. When it hit, I heard it make the noise of something small shattering into a million pieces.

From my perch high above them, I saw the men jump up and look in the direction of my broken Hawkeye, then I saw Mr. Leo Choplin come running. "Don't move!" he yelled. "Stay right there! I'm coming!"

The ladder shook with Mr. Choplin's weight as he climbed up to me. I wanted to disappear, to dissolve into space, but instead, like the brides appearing in my father's developing tray, I had suddenly materialized for everybody. At last he was next to me, his arm protectively around my back. Up close, when he saw my face, he recognized me and smiled. "Well, the photographer," he said. "Trying to steal my act?"

"Oh, no," I insisted. "I don't have flashbulbs. I could never take a picture at night like you can."

He frowned. "I don't think you'll be able to take any more pictures in the daytime now, either." We both looked down at the men picking up the pieces of my Hawkeye. Even from there we could see the long strip of exposed useless film.

"I was just trying to get a picture of my house from here," I told him.

"And which house would that be?"

I pointed, and he nodded.

"Well, I'll make sure I get that house tonight. How about that."

"And there's my friend Gayle's house. And my school, and the pool."

But now he was ignoring me. "Let's get you down from here."

Mr. Choplin helped me down off the water tower, keeping a step ahead of me all the way. By the time we touched ground, the men had gathered up my camera in a bag and gave it to me. I looked inside and wanted to cry.

Mr. Choplin tried to make me feel better by showing me how all his equipment would work. He explained how he'd be using three different cameras, opening their shutters in the darkness and then sending out a giant flash, and then after the flash, closing the shutters. He told me how he'd be aiming at different angles all over. And how Sylvania had supplied all the bulbs. There were nearly fifteen hundred bulbs, and he was planning to take seventy photographs in all. He even explained about the magnesium foil in the flashbulbs, but then the men were done with lunch and ready to get to work. Mr. Choplin shook my hand and sent me on my way. With my bag full of camera parts.

I didn't tell either of my parents about the camera till late that night. We were all sitting out back, even my brother, Douglas, watching the flashes from the water tower, trying to guess which of the flashes were for us. I imagined a photo of us, sitting there in our backyard, Mom and Dad on their metal lawn chairs, and me and Douglas on a blanket beside them. Douglas got tired about ten-thirty, and my mother put him to bed. She came back out for a little bit, but she was tired, too, and said good night.

I moved up into the chair beside my father. And in the darkness—his face sometimes lit to the brightness of daylight for brief seconds—I told him how I had climbed the water tower that day and that I had taken pictures of our house, Gayle's, the school, and everything, and then how

I had dropped my camera. I told him about Leo Choplin helping me down.

My father didn't say anything, and his not saying anything was terrible, worse than yelling. My eyes started to blur, but I didn't wipe them because I didn't want him to know. Finally he started to talk.

"You know, once I had a photo assignment. It was this big anniversary party with a lot of important people, and I was the only photographer allowed in. Even photographers from *Newsday* and the *Long Island Press* weren't invited, just me. Because I had done someone's wedding that they knew and they thought I was good and that I didn't get in the way too much. I took pictures all night. I was so excited."

"Which pictures are those?" I asked, sniffling and wiping my eyes with relief. I thought of his album that he'd show new customers.

"They don't exist."

"But didn't you say you took them?"

"Sure I took them, but when I went to develop

them, something went wrong. I don't know if it was the film, or the chemicals, or what, but there was nothing. Black. Nothing. Lost photographs. After all that work, and all that excitement."

"Like the pictures I took today."

He shook his head. "It's the worst thing that can happen to a photographer."

"Yeah," I whispered. "It sure is."

Suddenly I realized there hadn't been any flashing for a while. We were sitting in the dark. And it had been dark for a long time. The water tower loomed off in the distance, still and black against the stars.

"I sure hope he got our picture sitting here," I said.

"Well, if *he* didn't, surely these guys will." My father pointed over the lawn where lightning bugs were flashing. "Smile for them," he said, beginning to laugh and stretch.

I leaped from the lawn chair onto the grass. I held my arms wide and curtsied until a lightning bug flashed. I laughed and changed my pose. I wrapped my arms around myself and held a leg up like a crane. Another flash! I did a backroll into a handstand and collapsed. A flash! Over and over the lightning bugs took our pictures, me rolling and laughing in the grass late at night, my father smiling and folding up the chairs.

Of course those pictures never came out. Must have been the chemicals they used, or maybe they dropped their cameras heading home, but that's okay. Even without pictures, I'll remember every bit of it.

DEAD FLIES

1966

I'm Tommy LaRocca, and as soon as I'm old enough I'm getting outta Levittown for good. I'm leaving this town.

Oh, you don't really mean that, Tommy.

Watch me. Maybe I'll go to Vietnam like my brother, Chick. I won't even wait to get drafted, or maybe I'll go to Canada like my cousin Eddie, or maybe I'll go to California where Chick said it's always warm and the girls are all movie stars and everyone drives convertibles. Anything's gotta be better than Levittown.

Aw, it's not that bad.

Anyway, this here is my friend, Flytrap Klinkenburg. He was six feet tall by the time he was seven and probably wouldn't have any friends except that he has a way with flies.

That's not true at all. I wasn't six feet tall until I was in junior high. But it is true I was always a head or two taller than everybody else. And the part about the flies is true. Yeah, that's true.

And he won't tell us how he does the fly trick.

I did too. I showed you, Tommy. You take a rubber band and stretch it over the tip of your finger like this, pull it around your hand, and cap it on your thumb. Then when you see a fly passing by, you close one eye, aim, and bing!

Not *that* fly trick. The other one. Where you put a fly on a leash.

Oh.

See! He won't tell anyone. It's his big secret.

Remember that time, Tommy, remember that time in sixth grade when I hit the fly over Mrs.

Dillback's desk and the dead fly and rubber band landed on her book while she was calling attendance?

What I want to know is how you did it that time when you had us bring you live flies in tissues or jars. And the next morning you brought them in all tame and on string leashes.

See? He just smiles. We'll never know. But I saved my flies. They're dead now, but I have three dead flies still on their string leashes at home in my drawer. I won't let my mother throw them out. She'll have to wait till I leave. Then I'll forget all about them.

I probably won't remember anything about living here, either. It's the most boring place in the world. I'll forget the name of my street as soon as I leave it. And when I'm living in some nice warm place with palm trees and ocean drives, you'll ask me how I liked Levittown and I'll probably say, "Levittown? Where's that?"

Tommy's got a rotten attitude, and my mom says he's gonna be in big trouble if he keeps it up. She doesn't like me to hang out with him after school. But I know Tommy. He's a lot of talk. And me, I think I'll stay in Levittown forever.

You would.

Tommy's big brother, Chick, told us I'll probably be too tall to get drafted, 4F he called it. My dad says that by the time I'm old enough to be drafted, the war will be over so don't worry.

So I don't worry. And I could tell you a million things I'll never forget about Levittown.

Name one.

The day Kennedy was shot.

Hmph.

Right. See? You'll remember stuff. It was a Friday and we were just back from lunch, all sweaty after playing wall ball, and the principal came to our teacher.

That's not the way it happened at all. There was an announcement over the PA system and the principal asked all the teachers to report to the office immediately, and Mrs. Ward let Grace Dibble be monitor and take down names of anyone who talked while she was gone.

Oh, yeah. And then *she came back and told us.*

No. Then she came back to the class and stood in the doorway and Miss Gear was there and they were whispering together and Miss Gear started to cry.

I'd forgotten that.

Of course you did, colander-brain.

Anyway, they were standing in the doorway and I'd never seen Miss Gear cry before and we all got real quiet. Mrs. Ward even hugged her before she came into the room. I got scared. I remember in second grade when Larry Franklin's mom died. That was terrible.

So she comes into the room and stands in front of the class. Her eyes were all red and her hands were shaking, and you could have heard a paper clip drop. Man, it was weird to see her like that. She was usually kind of strict and mean—

She was not *mean.*

She was always mean to me. Anyway, she stood there and told us that President Kennedy had been shot and that he was dead.

A couple of girls started crying. Then she told us that school was closing and we were all to go right home.

We should've gone right home.

I did.

I mean I should've. I never should've gone to your house.

Remember how the janitor was pulling the flag halfway down the pole when we left? And people passing in cars were yelling to each other, "Is it true? Is it true?"

I remember how glad your brother was to get outta high school early and how he was working under the hood of some broken-down car in your driveway, saying how they should shoot all the presidents everywhere. That they were all bums and should be hung. Or that they should put all the leaders in an arena and make them fight to the death. And whoever was left would be king of the world.

Chick said that?

You don't remember?

No, I just remember about the trees. I remember how my mother wasn't home and how the three of us ate leftover chicken and potato chips and then we followed Chick outta the house because we had nothing else to do and he always seemed to be on some kind of a mission.

He wrecked the fruit trees.

He used to be so angry all the time.

He put all his weight into the tree until it bent over and then he stomped on it, stomping and stomping until it cracked near the base, and then he'd go on to the next tree in line.

Who'd those trees belong to, anyway?

I don't know. They were between houses, planted when all these houses were first built. The builder's grandfather or some old man planted them. Abraham Levitt. Wasn't that it?

Who knows. We sure did get in trouble.

Yeah. We never shoulda gone back to try and fix them.

Dumb old trees. Who cares. Who cares about dumb old fruit trees. I'd rather have Chick back in our driveway any day. I'd knock down a hundred fruit trees if it would bring him back right this minute. Even if he did think I was a pesty brother. Even if he did think you were a stupid, big dummy kid. I'd do anything.

Don't say that, Tommy.

Get lost, Flytrap.

Please don't say that, Tommy. How about this? How about I show you how to put a fly on a leash? Go get some string and some little pieces of straw. And I'll show you, Tommy. Go ahead now. I'll show you.

THE LONGEST

SUMMER ON RECORD

1978

Imagine the longest summer vacation in the history of the universe, a summer vacation that lasts longer than July and August. One that goes on and on, clear through the weeks of September and October. It happened here in Levittown, and my father made me keep a diary to prove it.

I'm Suzanne Stapleton, and those months I missed were because of a teachers' strike, when I would've been in sixth grade. Some of my friends' parents forced them to go to school, where there were substitutes and other parents pretending to be "teachers." Seeing as how my dad's a teacher at Merrick High School, and my mother's a school librarian in Lynbrook, they said they would honor the strike and they made us stay home.

This also involved my sister, Caroline, who was in fourth grade, and in some indirect ways, my little brother, Peter, who was four and hadn't started nursery school yet.

So here are some entries from my diary during those months. And by the way, I named my diary *Leonora Baptista.*

Wednesday, September 6, 1978

Dear Leonora Baptista,

This is the best year ever. The teachers at my school are on strike, and summer will just go on and on until they come back. My parents had to go back to their schools, so this past weekend Grampy drove Grammy out from Queens, and she'll be taking care of us.

My parents gave Grammy their bedroom down-stairs, and Mom and Dad sleep on the pullout sofa down in the living room. They did this so that when they leave early in the morning they don't have to wake her up, but she got up this morning anyway and made them pancakes. I heard Mom tell Dad that she'd rather have grapefruit and toast.

Grammy let me go to Lori's house today. Lori's my best friend in the entire world and gets to stay home alone most of the day. Her father works in the city, and her mother works at Adelphi University, and she doesn't have any little brothers or sisters. But she has to call her mother at work every hour on the hour. We went over to the pool, thinking we'd swim and hang out there all day, but the pool was closed. I forgot. Labor Day was the end of the pool. So we put nail polish on our fingers and our toes, and watched a movie on TV about giant ants in the Midtown Tunnel.

I will write more tomorrow.

Sunday, September 10, 1978

Dear Leonora,

First Dad insists that Caroline and I keep our diaries every day. And now Mom comes up with the idea that Caroline and I have to do all the dishes every night. And get this—we have to alternate doing the dishes. If it's my turn, I have to do the whole thing—clear the table, wash and dry, and Caroline has to read to me. And then the next night, it's Caroline's turn and I read.

Sounds dumb. I did the dishes and Caroline read. She picked Charlotte's Web. *I had forgotten about that story.*

Wednesday, September 13, 1978

Dear Leonora,

Grammy is cooking all the time. I think she's driving Mom nuts. She has rearranged all the cabinets so Mom can't find anything. Grammy says when the strike is over, Mom can put everything back the way she likes it, but as long as she's chief cook and bottle washer, she'll keep them the way that's handy for her. As far as bottle washer goes, I don't know where she got that. Tonight Caroline washed and I read. Mom brought home a pile of books. I picked Julie of the Wolves *to read.*

Mom says we'll all be fat by the time the strike is over. Grammy made chocolate-walnut cookies at lunchtime, which were wonderful, but then she also made a strange coleslaw with peanuts and tangerines in it....

Friday, September 15, 1978

Dear Leonora,

We went shopping this morning, walked with Grammy over to the stores. She let me buy two goldfish and a bowl. Actually it's for me and Caroline. Caroline named hers Hungry. Mine has longer fins and I named him Budapest.

Grammy also bought some wool and a hook and she's teaching me how to crochet. I'll make an afghan once I've got the stitches down pat.

There's not much else to write. Caroline read some Charlotte's Web *on her own, so after dinner she skipped a big part. Now I have to read to catch up. We promised each other we wouldn't do that anymore. Whatever becomes a dish-washing book stays in the kitchen by the toaster.*

Tuesday, September 19, 1978

Dear Leonora,

So sorry I haven't written in a while. There's just nothing else to write. Went to Lori's and we braided each other's hair and tried on her mother's dresses and some of her underwear. Lori is much skinnier than I am. I feel fat. It must be Grammy's brownies.

The afghan is getting pretty big. Grammy says I'm a natural. I love doing it. When I start, I can't stop. I keep thinking, one more round, one more round.

Friday, September 22, 1978

Dear Leonora,

It was raining hard this morning, and Lori's mother dropped her off here. We ended up playing "train." Of course we're a little old for that, but Dad asked me this morning to spend some time with Caroline and Peter. We lined up all the dining room and kitchen chairs and even made tickets. Peter was so cute. Sometimes he was the engineer, putting oil in the wheels, and other times he was the commuter, reading his newspaper. He kept saying, "All aboard for Baltimore! All aboard for Baltimore!" Grammy made us soup. Usually she does the lunch dishes, but she let us do them so Lori could read to us. Then we made the chairs into a barn shape and played Charlotte's Web.

Monday, September 25, 1978

Dear Leonora,

I'm back. So sorry I haven't written for a couple of days. Grampy was here this weekend, so we had a full house.

Bad news. Lori's mom says the strike is going on too long and that Lori has to go back to school. So she went this morning and I missed her. I wanted to walk with her, but Mom says no. She doesn't want me near the school. There are picket lines. And we heard school bus windows were broken. So it was a boring day. I started reading the pile of books Mom brought home from work. I read the first page in each book and then I picked. I'm reading A Wrinkle in Time.

Mom also brought books for Peter, and we all had a good laugh this afternoon when Grammy started to read him one of the Lyle Crocodile books and Peter pulled a chair up to the sink and started to wash the dishes!

Thursday, September 28, 1978

Dear Leonora,

Mom and Dad seem worried about the strike. They come home each day and read the papers and make phone calls and argue. They don't argue with each other. They actually agree with each other, but they get all stormed up over what's going on and their voices get loud. Dad says that someday the teachers and the board members will come to an agreement and shake hands, but neighbors will still be furious with each other.

Mom spoke to Lori's mother over the phone, and later I heard her whispering to Dad that Lori cries herself to sleep each night. And that her teacher is a substitute from the city and she yells all the time. There were even mounted police at school. The good part about that news is that Mom asked Mrs. Friedman to let Lori stay with us for the rest of the strike. She said she had a plan. I didn't hear what the plan was, but if I know Mom, it probably has to do with Lori joining our dish-washing jobs or something. Mrs. Friedman said she'd think about it.

Monday, October 2, 1978

Dear Leonora,

I walked to within two blocks of school this afternoon and met Lori coming home. We found a big box at the curb over on Periwinkle Road. It was left over from someone's new console TV and once we got it in the living room, we found out that all of us could fit in it—me, Lori, Caroline, and Peter. We had just seen a show last night about hot-air balloons, so we pretended we were floating out over the countryside. Then we hit a storm and we all had to sit down while the box rocked and bucked. When the storm cleared, we stood up and had no idea where we were. We were out over an ocean. Caroline is so dramatic. She pretended she was crying and she would say, "Oh, where are we? Where are we? Will we ever get home again?" And Peter yelled, "All aboard for Baltimore!"

Wednesday, October 4, 1978

Dear Leonora,

Oh, what a wonderful plan! A most spectacular, terrific, incredible plan! We had school today in our dining room! And Mr. Batorski came! He's going to be our teacher when the strike is finally over. I've never had a man teacher before and I was a little nervous about it, but he's great. Six kids from my class came. Including Lori! Mom had called all their mothers, and she said she had checked with the union, and called Mr. Batorski, and he's going to come every morning until the strike is over.

Today he brought a big globe with him and we

played hot potato with it. He would sing old rock-and-roll songs and when he stopped, whoever was holding the globe had to freeze and check where their ten fingers were. They could pick one finger and write or draw or make something about that place. Lori was all excited because two of her fingers were on Mexico and she went there last summer, so tomorrow she's going to bring in all her Mexican stuff to tell us about. My fingers weren't on anywhere I'd ever been, so I picked a word that sounded interesting. Amman. I don't know anything about Amman. So I'll go to the library and do some research.

Mr. Batorski just stayed the morning, but Mom had said the kids could read any of the books she'd brought home, as long as they read them at our house. If Grammy said it was okay. So a couple of the girls stayed and read. We spread out on the dining room floor under the table. It was very quiet, and Grammy brought us a dish of cookies, with of all things in them—M&M's.

•   •   •

Thursday, October 19, 1978

Dear Leonora,

Oh, I'm so, so sorry I'm not writing every day. But I've been pretty busy with some schoolwork. Mr. Batorski brought pen pals for all of us, so we were writing letters, and then Peter had an earache, and it turned out he was getting chicken pox, so Mom had to take off from school for a few days and we had to have our classes at Lori's, where her mother wasn't home, but she said it would be all right if Grammy came along and supervised everything.

I heard Mom laughing one night on the phone, and later she told Dad that Grammy had rearranged Lori's kitchen.

Monday, October 30, 1978

Dear Leonora,

The strike is over! We can go back. And just in time for Halloween. Mr. Batorski had told us that even if the strike lasted until Christmas, he wanted us all to wear costumes to his class the first day back. So Grammy baked Halloween cupcakes after dinner and put an orange candy witch on top of each one. After our baths and everything, we discovered about six of the witches were gone. Peter. He said he didn't take them and that we could even check down his throat, but you could see the little orange bits in his teeth when you looked, so Grammy made him put candy corn on the bare cupcakes, and she kept saying, "Oh, somebody will be so sad not to get a witch on their cupcake. What a shame." Peter was real quiet, and finally he said, real sad, "What a pity by you. I'm so sad for it."

So here I am in bed, Leonora. Mom said I can write for just a bit and then I have to turn the light out and get to sleep. I don't think I'll be able to sleep tonight. Grammy's staying on till Friday night, when Grampy will come for her. I think Mom will spend the weekend rearranging the kitchen and getting things back the way she likes them. And then next week Peter will start his nursery-school program.

I read eleven books while I was off, and learned

about Amman and photosynthesis and the Homestead Act, and Mom has promised us we can keep doing the dishes together just like during the strike. I'm glad, because we're in the middle of The Diary of Anne Frank.

I can't believe how nervous and excited I am. I was so glad we didn't have to go to school in September, so glad that our vacation turned out to be so long, but now I'm glad to be going back, too. Glad Mr. Batorski is my new teacher. Glad Lori and I can walk to school together. Glad that everything's going to be normal again.

Well, I'd better try to sleep. Good night, Leonora. And don't go away. I'll be back tomorrow.

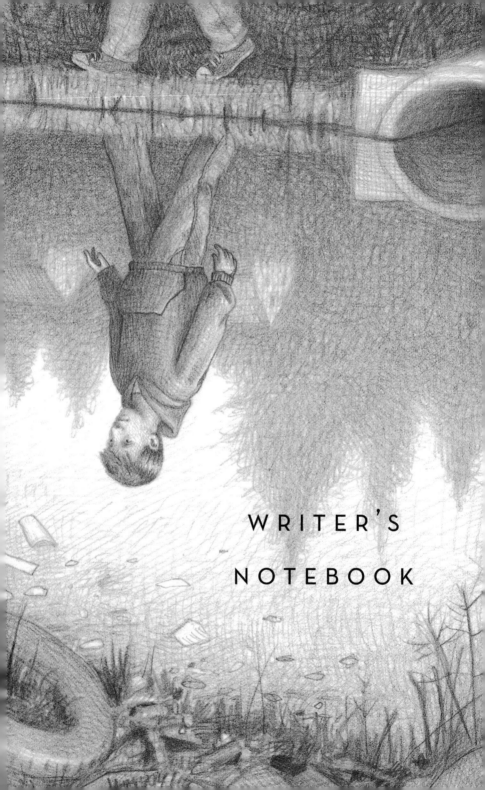

WRITER'S

NOTEBOOK

1983

You could probably say that Levittown shapes the way kids around here think, and that because I'm growing up here, I wear Levittown-tinted glasses and see everything through those lenses. But I learned from my teacher, Mrs. Mehlman, that although things may look a certain way from here, if I were to walk around and look at the same thing from another angle, I'd see a whole different world.

My name is Jeremy Nichols and I want to be a

writer when I grow up. If I were a writer, I would use my books to show this feeling I have about things being more complicated than they seem on the surface. Maybe I'd even be able to show how a single thing can be both good and bad, and that life is never simple.

But I'm learning that writing isn't easy, either. You can't just blurt out everything in your head onto a piece of paper. There are tools you've got to learn to use, just like if you wanted to be an architect or a dentist.

This year Mrs. Mehlman taught us how to keep writers' notebooks and I write in mine all the time. It helps me with my thinking, and it's awesome how much I have to write about. Mrs. Mehlman collects our notebooks once a week and writes comments.

The first section in my writer's notebook is called THEMES. In here I write all the things that bother me, things that I worry about, things that seem to have no answers. At the top of each page in this section, I write stuff like—

> a) *Sometimes it seems as though people who are different will never get along.*
> b) *What about pollution?*
> c) *Can a person be totally honest, no matter what?*

Then Mrs. Mehlman writes things like—

> What do you mean by "people who are different"?
> What kind of pollution?
> What's your definition of honesty?

She signs it Mrs. M.

So later, usually at night, because that's when my thoughts seem the loudest and the worries the hardest, I go back to those questions and write on them some more. For instance, for the first one, I wrote:

I think a lot lately about white people and black people getting along. Just the other night my mother was saying how here in Levittown when the houses were first built, there was a clause in the deeds that said you could never sell one of these houses to someone who wasn't Caucasian. So all the black soldiers who came back from fighting in WWII weren't allowed to live here. They were turned away.

Mom says it's fear that makes some people think up things like that, fear that people who are different from you can somehow take something away from you or keep you from getting what you want. And I notice there still aren't many black families around here.

That's a lot to think about, Jeremy.
Mrs. M.

The next page is about pollution. I guess I worry

about pollution because it's all around me. There's no getting away from it. The water, the air, everything. And I worry if anything can be done. This is what I wrote on my pollution page:

> *If everything all around you for miles and miles is polluted, what good does it do to clean up the little spot where you are?*

Can you think of an example of this, Jeremy? Can you be specific? Mrs. M.

I thought of the sump right away. And something that actually happened here in Levittown in one of our sumps last year when I was in the fourth grade. To write about it I'd have to use what I wrote in my SETTING section.

This is where I write about the places where stories could happen. Here. Check it out.

THE SUMPS
Not every town has them. But Levittown

does. A sump is just a piece of wild land where the street drains empty after a rain. So it looks like a nice pond, except when you look close you see it's fed water by big concrete pipes. The town put a chain-link fence around our sumps long ago. Nobody's actually allowed to go in them, but kids around here have always played there, and I don't ever remember anyone being sent away. The paths through the holes in the fences are worn smooth, and some of the holes are so wide you can get your dirt bike in for the days when you have races.

Sometimes sumps can be pretty pol-luted looking—a dumping place for old furniture, abandoned car parts, and other garbage. But some can be nice, depend-ing on how people take care of them.

I'll bet some pretty terrific adventures could happen here. Mrs. M.

* * *

The next important section in my writer's notebook is called CHARACTERS. These are the people that will be in my stories someday. I love this part. It's like making up new friends and figuring out exactly what they might be like if you were to meet them. These are some characters I've been working on:

> *Timmy. Little white boy about seven years old. He wears old sneakers, T-shirts that are too big for him. He's got real orange freckles on his face, and he wears a Yankees hat backwards. He really looks up to his older brother and wants to be just like him.*

Jeremy, why do you say he's a *white* boy? Mrs. M.

> *Andy. Timmy's older brother, about eleven. He's one of those kids who's good*

at everything he does. He's strong, fast, smart. He can shoot baskets, spit bubbles, and ride his dirt bike faster than anybody. He can also do neat things like catch frogs and make them be still.

Spit bubbles!?! Mrs. M.

Tyrone. I want him to be a black kid, and he and Andy are best friends. He's got a dirt bike, too. But he's a computer genius at school and always talking about how someday he's going to invent a computer that would fit in your pocket....

Later, when Mrs. Mehlman hadn't commented on this, I added:

Mrs. M., how come you didn't ask me why I said Tyrone was a black boy and you asked why I said Timmy's a white boy?

Good point, Jeremy. I'll think about that.
Mrs. M.

Mr. Anderson. Tyrone's father. He's a sci-
ence teacher and whenever he's with
Tyrone and Tyrone's friends, he tries to
teach them stuff, like if they're out at
night, he points out the constellations, or
he explains the spin on a basketball and
how you can make it work for you.

So those are the ingredients that you need to
begin a story—a setting, some people to put in the
setting, and something you're kind of worried
about or thinking about a lot. I asked Mrs.
Mehlman if I can use all these parts with a true
experience. She said why not. She told me to see
if I could come up with a "what if" for my WHAT
IF section. This is what I decided on. And this
was true.

What if Timmy, Andy, and Tyrone decide

to clean up a really polluted sump, and they keep it a secret from their parents because they think they're not allowed, but when the parents find out, they actually join in?

Wow, Jeremy. Go for it! Mrs. M.

I'll bet you never realized how much thinking and preparation go into a story, did you? Well, now that I've done some of this think work, I'm ready to start my story in my MANUSCRIPT IN PROGRESS section. This is what I have so far:

It was a hot summer day. Timmy's hands were wet and full of spring guppies. He was standing knee-deep in the sump by a concrete pipe. He had his sneakers on because of the broken glass.

Suddenly his brother called to him from the top of the hill. "Look at this,

Timmy! Come here!" Timmy dropped the guppies and scrambled up the hill.

Andy showed Timmy what he had in his hands—a frog, one that filled his two cupped hands. And it was struggling to jump away.

"Watch this," Andy said. He stepped back and began to whip his arm in big circles, faster and faster, like he was winding up for a pitch, but the frog was in his hand. He stopped suddenly and held it out. The frog was still, his front and back legs limp, all dizzy and stunned. His tongue was hanging out.

"Wow!" Timmy said. "That's the best! I'll trade you." And out of his pocket Timmy pulled a small turtle shell. Andy took the shell without a word and held it up to the sun to peer into it. He handed over the stunned frog.

Suddenly they heard Tyrone call and

saw him coming through the cut in the chain-link fence.

"Tyrone, look what Andy did!" Timmy held out the frog to show him, but the frog had regained his senses and from Timmy's open hand it leaped high in the air and disappeared into the tall grasses. "No fair! No fair!" he started yelling, and he ran after it.

"Where's your bike, Tyrone?" Andy asked. "I thought we were going to race today."

Tyrone frowned and shook his head. "My dad won't let me bring it here anymore. Too much broken glass," he said.

Andy hated to agree, but it was true. "Yeah. I've had three flats so far this summer. My mother keeps asking where I'm riding that there's so much glass."

Andy and Tyrone stood there and looked around at their sump. It was pretty awful, and dangerous, too. There was an *old stuffed chair, an abandoned car chassis, a dead battery, and some busted crates. Not to mention the broken glass that was rough on their tires.*

Andy thought it was pretty hopeless and then all of a sudden, Tyrone said, "Hey! Why don't we clean it up?"

Excellent beginning, Jeremy. Mrs. M.

Yeah, beginnings are easy. It's the endings that can be murder. Like how much of the truth can I tell? How honest can I be? Because the truth is that the kids around here *did* clean up the sump and the parents really did chip in, but the bigger truth is that running across the sky over the sump, casting their shadows on the water tower and over the wild cherry trees in the sump, are giant steel towers with high power lines as thick as my leg. My mom says they might be creating worse pollution than any littered sump.

So it's not easy being a writer. I've already filled

out four whole notebooks! And I could probably spend the rest of my life trying to figure out if a writer can ever be totally honest. I hope that what Mrs. Mehlman says is true—that a fiction writer makes up lies in order to tell a greater truth— because I really believe that like the families at the sump, most people want to work together to make the world a better place. And it really is possible for a black boy and a white boy to be best friends. I like to think this is the greater truth she's talking about.

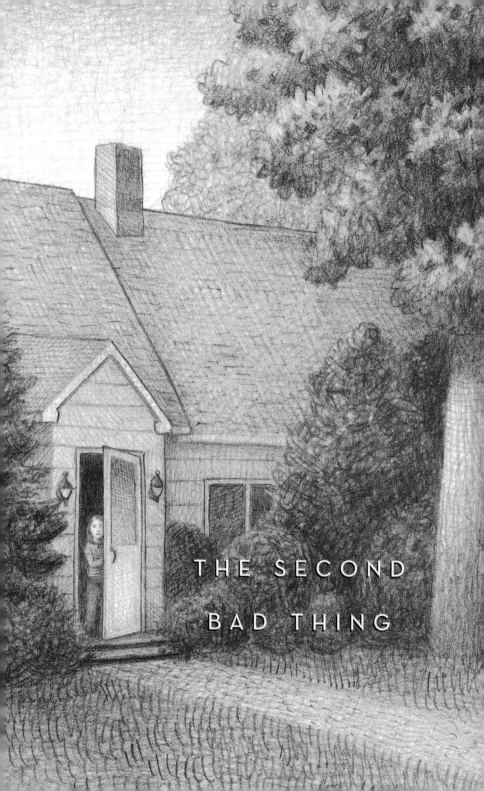

THE SECOND

BAD THING

1996

Grandma used to say that bad things come in threes. So when she died two years ago, I braced myself for the two bad things I was sure would be coming. At first I thought Daddy losing his job and having to go back to college was one of those bad things. And that my grandfather coming to live with us was the third.

But Grandma also used to say that hindsight is twenty-twenty, which means you can see real good when you're looking back at things. And I can say for sure now that those things weren't bad at all, that some "bad things" have an odd way of turning good on you, like a hard green banana grows soft and yellow while you're not watching it.

No, there was only one other "bad thing" that happened that year, and no matter how much hindsight I ever have, there's no way that it could ever be made good.

My name is Katie Bachman. I'm twelve now, and I live in Levittown. Last year there were six of us, me, my parents, my grandfather, who we all call Otto, my brother Buster, who was born a year before me, and Harrison, the surprise baby my parents had that fall.

It was late November when Otto left his home in South Carolina and moved in with us. I remember we were having the beginnings of an early snowstorm the day he walked through the front door. Daddy was behind him carrying his luggage, and Mom was standing there, all proud and excited, holding Harrison. Buster had just come down the stairs from his room.

It had been a couple of years since Buster and I had seen Otto, but I could tell even then things weren't going to be easy. Otto didn't have his jacket off. He hadn't even gotten his first look at Harrison when he said to Buster, "What'd they do? Burn down the Levittown barber shop?"

I knew Buster felt shy about his hair, about the way he had let a long tail grow down the back of his neck like some of his friends, but he didn't say anything. He just sort of ducked his head, his ears grew bright, and in a heartbeat, while Mom showed Otto where he'd be staying, Buster disappeared back up to his room.

Daddy followed Mom and Otto with the suitcases. "We've been using this added side room as a sort of den or TV room, Otto," he was saying, "but this'll be your room for the time being, and as soon as the weather gets warmer, we'll start building an extension out back."

I had known from this end of a hundred phone conversations that Otto was moving up to live with us because he was all alone now that Grandma was gone, and also because he had some money from a house sale. My family—once Dad lost his job—had less and less money, but we had plenty of company to offer. The deal was, Otto would help with the bills, in exchange for the pleasure of our company....

It seemed like a tall order to me. And Otto didn't look too excited, either. "Let's not do anything rash," he said. "There'll be plenty of time for us to decide."

I had watched and listened that afternoon as Otto unpacked and told my mother about how icy the roads were up here in New York, and how warm it was right then in South Carolina. Harrison had started to fuss, so they all moved into the kitchen where the food was almost ready.

Even after all this time I can still remember the exact feel of the cold winter that day, beating up against the windows in the den, and the distant thumping beat of Buster's stereo cranked up. It makes me smile now, just as it did then. It was his old *Dirty Dancing* tape, and without looking I knew he was lip-synching and dancing in front of the mirror like we used to do.

Day by day things between Otto and Buster went from bad to worse. They didn't give each other half a chance. It was as though the way Buster breathed irritated Otto, and it wasn't long before the way Otto cast a shadow when he stood near the lamp drove Buster nuts. They reminded me of my friend Chrissie's cats. She has two cats that get along fine, but one day we added a third and it was like an explosion went off in her house. There were cats spitting from the chandelier, cats growling under the chairs, cats running along the walls, cats pouncing from tops of bookcases, cats skittering across rugs, backs arched, fur flying. Otto and Buster were making all of us a little nuts.

We discovered pretty early that although Buster and Otto got along like a sack full of cats, Otto had a way with Harrison. Mom and Dad had told us that Mom would go back to work as soon as Dad started his college classes, but they weren't sure who would take care of Harrison—until the day he got his DPT shots.

Mom brought him home from the doctor's that day and spent an hour pacing the floor. Harrison screamed like he had a sleeper full of hornets. It didn't put Mom in much of a good mood, so I slipped out and went to Chrissie's. We played Monopoly and I stayed over there as long as I could, until her mother was putting their dinner out, until when I finally headed home the sky was a smooth purple sheet with the trees like clear black scribbles pressed up against it.

I was surprised when I walked in the back door. It was strangely quiet. There were some pots simmering on the stove, and Mom was at the table reading *Newsday*. When I looked over her shoulder, I saw she was reading the job ads.

"Hi, honey," she said without looking up.

"Where's Harrison?" I asked.

She motioned with her chin toward the

shadowed living room. I tiptoed toward the door and looked in. Otto was in the middle of the room, sitting in the wooden rocking chair with Harrison lying across his lap. They were both motionless, frozen. Otto looked up at me.

"He sleeping?" I whispered.

Otto nodded and at that slight movement, Harrison let out a pitiful wail.

"They have to be very still after their DPT shots," Otto said, smoothing a blanket tighter around Harrison. "It's sort of like a bad hangover. He just has to be very, very still." Otto himself grew still, his thin hand spread gently across the baby's legs, and Harrison quieted.

I stayed there awhile, next to them, thinking how Otto was like two different people, one way with Buster and another with Harrison, and the three of us barely breathed.

It wasn't long after that, after a tense and all-around grouchy dinner, when Otto disappeared into the den and Buster locked himself in his room. I saw Mom look across the kitchen table at Dad and sigh. Harrison was mushing some leftover peaches into his high-chair tray, and I had cleared my dishes away and opened my math homework in my place.

"I worry that this isn't going to work," Mom said.

Dad took off his glasses and rubbed his eyes. "I've never seen Buster this rude."

"It's not just Buster. Your father doesn't even try. Buster can't come into a room without your father picking on something about him—his clothes, his hair, his shoes, his fingernails. He never gets off his case. And you can't tell Otto anything."

"I know, I know." Dad shrugged. "Maybe they're too much alike. I don't know what to say. But something had better change soon."

Mom stood up and scooped Harrison from the high chair into her arms. "I just hope it happens before we start to build the extension."

Something would change all right. But not

what I had thought, sitting there doing my math homework. Not in a million years.

It was one of those warm Saturdays in March, when the day almost tricks you into thinking summer is just around the corner. There were a few piles of black and white hard snow here and there, but the streets were clear now, and most of the winter potholes were filled in. Up and down the blocks you could hear garage doors opening and dusty bikes being rolled out into the street. No one zippered their jackets, or even wore their bike helmets that day. As though bringing the bikes out was just a sudden and spontaneous event that swept everyone away.

Buster opened the front door and yelled in. "Katie! We're going over to the school yard to play ball. Wanna come?"

I was in the middle of baking my favorite sticky cinnamon buns that come in a tube. "Can you wait for me? I'll be a few minutes. Till these come out of the oven."

Buster slumped against the door and moaned. "Katie. They're waiting. We've got to get to the field first."

I slid the pan into the oven. "So, go! Go ahead. I'll catch up." Then I called, "Buster!" I think I wanted to remind him I had a flat tire on my bike, but he was gone.

From out of nowhere it seemed, Otto was standing at the front window looking out. "Where's he racing to now?"

"School yard," I answered, setting the timer.

"How come he doesn't use his real name?"

I wasn't sure I had heard him. "What, Otto?"

"I said, why doesn't that boy use his real name? How come he never says his name is Otto? What's this 'Buster' crap?"

"Why, we've never called him that, Otto. That's your name. How can we have two Ottos?"

"Lots of families have two Bills or two Toms. What's the big deal?"

I remember laughing. "Otto! You're insulted,

aren't you? You're upset 'cause Buster's got a nick-name. And he doesn't use yours. It's not his fault. No one's ever called him Otto."

"That's what he was named. That's the name on his birth certificate. That's what I was told. He was s'posed to be named for me."

I remember smiling at Otto, watching him, and taking a lick of the cinnamon bun icing. "Well, go tell him, Otto. Quick, before he's gone. Tell him you want to share a name with him and get every-body all mixed up. Tell him from now on his name is Otto."

But Otto ignored me and turned away from the window and the image of the three boys pedaling like crazy up the street.

Any one of us could have changed what hap-pened. We each thought of things we could have done different, things that might have altered things one way or the other by a few minutes. Otto must've thought how he should've called

Buster back to tell him to use his real name, how
then Buster would've gotten to the overpass a little bit later.

I kept thinking if only I had insisted Buster
wait for me. Maybe he would have gotten to the
overpass ten minutes later. Or maybe I could have
left the cinnamon buns for Otto to finish and I
would've been on Buster's handlebars. I would
have slowed him down, and he never would have
tried to cut around.

Buster's friend Nick said he'd thought about
his bike helmet, but didn't want everyone leaving
without him while he went to look for it. So at
exactly the wrong speed, my brother and his two
friends took off for the school yard down exactly
the wrong road without their helmets.

I wrote a poem about it. About how I imagine
it was. I keep it under my bed. I call it "Cutting
Around."

CUTTING AROUND
Nick and Jim and Buster head up the street.

On their bikes.
In that order. On their bikes.
Like kids at the end of the movie ET,
they should pedal up into the sky.
But Nick and Jim and Buster are on the ground,
wheels rolling on blacktop.
They're fast,
smooth slim legs pumping hard.
And Buster hates being last.
It's just the three of them in a line,
with Buster last.
They come to the overpass.
The road curves up before them—
an overpass so low you don't have to downshift
if your legs are strong.
So high you can't see what's coming.
Buster hates being last. And Buster cuts around.

Cuts around his two best friends,
not a mustache yet among them,
happy with a sudden warm day,
softballs in their back pockets,

a bat under Nick's arm,
and Buster cuts around. Buster cuts around,
wheels on blacktop,
sneakers on pedals,
laughing.

Oh, Buster, don't cut around.

They said later the car was going seventy in a thirty-mile zone. Some said Buster died on impact, stunned like a bird flying low across a highway. But some said he was still conscious when they slid the stretcher into the ambulance.

They said the driver of the car was drunk. And had no license. Just a girlfriend in the front seat—a girl who put her hands over her eyes when she saw Buster cut around, when she saw his hair, his brow, his surprised eyes cutting around.

So Buster never got to the school yard. He cut around, and he wouldn't have been able to cut around if I'd been on the handlebars. Dad says I mustn't think like that, but I heard him telling

Otto that he'd promised to take Buster to the boardwalk that day, and if he hadn't put it off till later, maybe Buster wouldn't have cut around. So I know we all had our things like that. Wondering what we could have done, what slight thing might have changed everything.

We had a funeral for my brother. A wake and a funeral that seemed to go on for days. I don't remember too much except that all my friends and Buster's friends from school were there, and seeing some of them cry made me cry. And all the grownups kept touching me and saying, "Are you okay? Are you okay?" Over and over.

Nick and Jim came back to the house after. The house was full of people who had brought casseroles and cakes, so we went up to my room and sat on the floor. We were all kind of quiet. There was nothing we wanted to do. No Monopoly. No Sega. No Uno. Nick kept crying, and we let him.

After a while, it started to get dark, and I

should have put a light on, but it was like I didn't want to move, and then there was a knock on my door.

It was Otto. He opened the door and looked in. He was holding Harrison on his hip, and Harrison started to kick and grin wildly when he saw Buster's friends there. "You guys okay?" Otto asked. I looked up at him and I saw his eyes were swollen and his fingers trembled around Harrison's belly.

I nodded, and he came into the room. "You guys? You're all right?" he said again.

"Yes, Mr. Bachman. We're okay."

He stood there looking at us. Sort of helpless. He seemed to be searching for something to say. "Have you kids learned anything from this?"

I thought right away of how I hadn't made Buster wait for me. How I'd never make cinnamon buns again.

But Nick said, "Yes, sir. To always wear my bike helmet." In my mind I could see Buster putting on his new black helmet and I could almost hear him saying it was cool. So cool.

"Yeah," Jim said softly. "And don't ride on the left side of the road. Especially going up a hill." I could see the back of Buster's neck under his helmet, his scrawny neck, and his tail of hair that was growing so long. And I knew suddenly what I had learned.

"If you love someone, tell them, before it's too late," I said.

When I looked up, Otto's eyes were red, like in a bad photograph. His face just seemed to collapse in on itself, and he didn't mind when I took Harrison out of his arms.

It's taken all this time, about two years, for us to be able to talk to each other and do things together, without Buster's shadow always darkening everything. Harrison helps. Little kids don't know too much about sadness, and he just keeps going along like a windup toy. It's also taken all this time for Dad to finally feel ready to lay the foundation for Otto's new room.

At first Dad thought they were going to have to rip up the cement that had been our patio, but then he decided that whoever did it did a fine job, and that it'll be able to stay as a part of the foundation. But there was still a lot of digging to do.

So early this past Saturday morning, we were all out there digging, even me and Mom. Harrison watched us from his old playpen set out in the morning sun. We borrowed sturdy shovels from all the neighbors around, and Tom Moran, our next-door neighbor, came over to help. He said he likes digging. Dad says *talking* is what he likes to do. And sure enough, no sooner had the digging begun than Mr. Moran took note of something and had to start talking about it.

"Why, take a look at this," he began, stopping his digging and peering at the patio foundation.

"Don't go telling me you see a crack, Tom," my father said, still digging. "I checked every inch of that slab, and it's perfect."

"No, no, not that," he answered. "There's

something here. You know, like a fossil, or an imprint or something."

I dug my shovel into the dirt and left it standing there. I went to see. Dirt had scattered over the patio, and Tom was gently dusting away a small patch. "Why, it says something. It's letters."

I got down on my hands and knees and helped brush away the dirt. Some stayed in the letters, making it easy to read. The letters were suddenly visible.

"What do you think that means?" I asked Mr. Moran.

"Darned if I know."

Otto came over to see. He took off his glasses and wiped his eyes and forehead with his sleeve. Then he put them back on and bent over close to the imprint. "Tee. Wee. T," he said. "Wonder who that was."

"You think it's somebody's name?"

"Looks that way to me," he said, pointing above the letters. There in the cement, right over the words TEEWEE T, was a set of footprints. Smallish. About my size. I stood and laid my sneakers over the imprints and they fit almost perfectly. "I wonder who TeeWee T was," I said.

"Let me think," Tom said, squinting off into space. "Before you lived here, there were the Jacksons. And I know just before them were the Fertshes. They were our first neighbors, but I don't know who was before them. I'm trying to think who would know. Maybe you could ask Mrs. Trezza. I think Andrew Trezza's parents were the original owners, and he bought the house from them when they retired to Florida. He's gone now, but maybe his widow might be able to tell you who lived here since the beginning."

I stood there in those footprints while everyone got back to work. The footprints faced the back of the house. I looked at the back windows and the back door and thought how this had once been someone named TeeWee T's home, and thinking this made my throat tighten as though I would cry.

If TeeWee T had been one of the original kids to live around here, that would have been in the forties, and this was the nineties. He'd be around sixty years old today. Almost like Otto.

I looked over at Otto, digging beside Daddy. I wondered if TeeWee T was a grandfather now, or if he was dead. I wondered if he had grown and lived a long life, or if he'd died young like Buster. Already I am taller than Buster had been when he died. Even my feet have grown bigger than his had been, and I hadn't realized it, but I grew right past a new pair of sneakers he had hardly worn. And then I wondered if Buster had ever pressed his name and the bottoms of his feet into wet cement.

"Daddy?" I said.

"Yes, honey." He didn't look up. His shovel lifted dirt and flung it. Lifted dirt and flung it.

"Are you going to pour wet cement for the rest of the floor?"

"That's the plan."

Then I knew what I had to do. I flew inside and

went to Harrison's room, what used to be Buster's room. Most of what is left of his stuff Mom packed away in the back of his closet, and I knew his sneakers were on the top of the piles. Mom says she means to give them to one of his friends, but just never does.

In the dark closet, when my hand found the sneakers, I suddenly thought I could smell Buster. It was so strong, I almost wanted to say something to him, or to reach out. Instead, I just sat down there in the darkness and waited. Until I couldn't smell him anymore.

The next day my father poured the fresh cement, and I wrote Buster's name in it. With my hands deep in his sneakers, I pressed my brother's footprints into the wet cement. And with a stick I wrote BUSTER/OTTO. Not that you'll be able to see any of it or anything once the flooring and the carpeting get laid down. But I know it's there. Along with TEEWEE T.

And maybe that's what neighborhoods are all

about. Always changing and growing and sometimes getting better, sometimes getting worse, but underneath it all, there are invisible footprints pressed into sidewalks and gardens and wet cement, footprints of all the kids who have ever played there. A kind of remembering that is everywhere. That can never go away.

BUSTER/OTTO

LAST,

THE MEMORIES

An epilogue

Today Levittown stretches in all directions, its boundaries lost in the borders of Hicksville, Wantagh, Westbury, and East Meadow. Mr. Levitt and his father, Abraham, would probably not recognize the town they once built and planted from scratch. Many of the houses are completely changed, with pillars and balconies, additions, cathedral ceilings, saunas, and skylights, looking for all the world as though they were built in the South or even California. The only original thing that remains in some of them is the paint inside the kitchen cabinets.

And the trees. There are still a lot of apple trees, and the pin oaks, maples, and oak trees have grown to line and shade the winding sidewalks. Sadly, the pear trees didn't make it, and most of the willows have blown over. But as sure as there are initials in concrete and old trees planted in neat rows, there is still Levittown—the families, the memories, the hard times, the good times.

If you look close enough at the chain-link fences that surround the town sumps, you will probably spot some holes as big as dirt bikes, and if you stop in at the library and find the display case, you will see for yourself that night photograph of Levittown, Levittown when it was young.

And no matter where you are right now, you can come on out and stand in the middle of it as the sun is going down, and you can know that right in the spot where you are standing, there used to be someone else, that at some other point in time, someone stood where you are standing,

ARTIST'S NOTE

————

BIOGRAPHIES

and

ACKNOWLEDGMENTS

ARTIST'S NOTE

by

BRIAN SELZNICK

I first met Pam Conrad in 1994, and we soon became friends. From the moment we were introduced, I adored being with her. Pam made me laugh, and her intelligence and curiosity were a constant source of inspiration. She was also my guide on an unforgettable tour of Levittown.

On December 21st, 1994, we visited all the spots she wrote about in the book. I brought two cameras with me just in case one didn't work, and I photographed the water tower, where the night photograph was taken in the 1950s, and the sump, which had indeed become overrun with junk just as Pam describes in the book. And of course, I photographed house after house. We were even able to find some houses that had not changed at all since the 1940s, but most of the houses had grown and transformed, just the way Pam describes so beautifully in the book.

Pam also took me to the Levittown Library, where I met the librarian, Maryann Donato, who showed us archival photos of the town's history. For reference, I photographed lots of these old photos and newspaper clippings, including a copy of that original night photograph, where the houses all glow like rows of spaceships in the black night.

Since another artist had already been commissioned to paint the jacket illustration for the orginal edition of the book, I was asked to create small pen-and-ink drawings to decorate the opening and closing of each chapter. With these simple little drawings, I tried to show how the town grew and changed.

When the book was released in October of 1995, I was delighted to be able to go back with Pam to the Levittown Library for a reading and a signing. Sadly, by that time, Pam had already been diagnosed with cancer, and she died several months later.

In this new edition of the book, many of the houses are the same houses I drew ten years ago, but the pictures themselves have grown to fill double-page spreads. Also, in the original drawings, we only saw the houses themselves. The children who lived inside them were left to the imagination. The most important thing that the book's editor, Tracy Mack, and the designer, David Saylor, encouraged me to do in this new edition, was draw the kids, because that's what this book is really all about.

This last fall, I returned to Levittown, by myself, to take more photographs and do further research for the new illustrations. It was a bright, sunny day, crisp and cool. I went back to the Levittown Library, I visited the Levittown Historical Museum, and I walked the curving streets of the town that Pam had loved so much. Her presense was everywhere and I thought a lot about her legacy.

At first, all I could focus on were all the books she would never get to write, because she had a world of stories inside her. She was one of those rare people who are true storytellers. But Pam once said that as long as her books are read, she'll be alive. I couldn't be more proud to have helped bring this work—one of *her* personal favorites—back to readers, where it belongs. Thank you for reading this book and helping to keep Pam's memory alive.

— Brian Selznick

Brooklyn, New York, April 2005

BIOGRAPHIES

PAM CONRAD grew up in Valley Stream, New York. "I believe in neighborhood," she once said about the inspiration for this book. "A place where families own their homes, where they work, play, make mistakes, and celebrate their lives." One of the most beloved authors for children and young adults, Conrad's treasured books include such classics as *Prairie Songs*, *Stonewords*, *My Daniel*, and *The Tub People*, illustrated by Richard Egielski. Her books have received numerous awards and distinctions, including the Edgar Allen Poe Award, *Boston Globe–Horn Book Magazine* Award Honors, Orbis Pictus Award Honors, ALA Best Books for Young Adults, NCTE Notables in Language Arts and Social Studies, and IRA Teachers' and Young Adult Choices.

BRIAN SELZNICK grew up in East Brunswick, New Jersey. "There were lots of kids on my block," he says. "We all played kickball and hide-and-seek and a game we called 'monster,' and when it snowed, we went sledding on the hill in my backyard. My mom still lives in that house, and even though it's changed a lot, it will always be home." Selznick is the award-winning illustrator of *Walt Whitman: Words for America* and the Caldecott Honor book *The Dinosaurs of Waterhouse Hawkins,* both by Barbara Kerley, as well as *When Marian Sang,* by Pam Muñoz Ryan. He lives in Brooklyn, New York.

ACKNOWLEDGMENTS

ACKNOWLEDGMENTS FROM THE ORIGINAL EDITION

I wish to acknowledge the generous help of so many people who have loved, and still love, Levittown: Mary Ann Donato, the children's librarian there; Janet Spar; Jane Pyres, the first baby to be born in Levittown, and her mother, Muriel Burke, who's in Florida now; their neighbor Harriet, who lives in Jamesport today; Ann Palaszczuk; Jane Howard; Eugene McCarthy's mother; Richard Herne, the cab driver who told me he lived in the best place in the world—Levittown; Josh Soren, a Levittown "scholar"; Bruce, who got in trouble there in the sixties; and Sey Chassler, who wrote an article for *Collier's* about the taking of the night photo of Levittown and, years later, was one of my writing teachers. (While a man named Leo Choplin really did take a night photo of Levittown, my account is entirely fictitious.)

I must also thank some special people who helped show me what it's like to live in Levittown today: James O'Garra, the librarian at Wisdom Lane School, and the wonderful bunch of Levittown kids he invited me to talk with—Steven Levy, Keri Brunnhoelzl, Jennifer Boyle, Alyse Anekstein, Nicole Gruenfelder, Elizabeth Martins, Shannon Ronan, Brian Sutch, Danny Durkin, Chris McGrath, Meghan Mitchell, Mary Dassaro, Melissa Galligan, and Jesse Halpern.

And there will never be the right words to thank Tracey Wall for sharing her memories of Ray with me.   —*Pam Conrad, 1995*

ACKNOWLEDGMENTS FOR THE 10TH ANNIVERSARY EDITION

I would like to thank Polly Dwyer, president of the Levittown Historical Society; Ann Glorioso, librarian, and Margaret Kapinos, children's librarian, both at the Levittown Public Library; Sarah Conrad; and Maria Carvainis.

And special thanks to everyone at Scholastic Press for bringing *Our House* back into print, especially David Saylor, Lillie Mear, Leslie Budnick, Liz Szabla, and two people who have been intimately involved with this book from the very beginning, Jean Feiwel and Tracy Mack.

—*Brian Selznick, 2005*

its green highlights lies in its toasty, buttery aromas and its remarkable balance on the palate. A wine that will benefit from a year or two in the cellar.

• Pierre Dupond, 235, rue de Thizy, 69653 Villefranche-sur-Saô ne, tel. 04.74.65.24.32, fax 04.74.68.04.14, e-mail p.dupond@seldon.fr

□
CH. FUISSE Les Brûlés 1999★★

1.8 ha 4,000 €15-23

Les Brûlés, a monopoly of Chateau Fuissé, owes its name to its full southern exposure that produces exceptionally mature grapes from which an eminent wine-maker, Jean-Jacques Vincent, knows exactly how to bring out the best. A brilliant green-gold colour, this elegant 99 has a fine, complex nose with oak and vanilla touches sustained by notes of ripe grapes and mild spices. On the palate it shows perfect balance and the oak is well-handled. It has good length. One taster felt it would go well with a sea-perch en croûte. A star was awarded to the famous cuvée **Vieilles Vignes 99**, which is still a touch reserved for the moment but has everything it needs to become a lovely wine in one to two years' time.

• SC Ch. de Fuissé, 71960 Fuissé, tel. 03.85.35.61.44, fax 03.85.35.67.34, e-mail jean-jacques.vincent@wanadoo.fr
• by appt.
• Jean-Jacques Vincent

□
DOM. DE FUSSIACUS
Vieilles vignes 1999★

2.5 ha 10,000 €11-15

This domaine reputedly takes its name from a Roman nobleman, popularly believed to be the founder of the village of Fuissé. This light yellow Vieilles Vignes 99 with bright glints has a touch of oakiness on the nose, opening out with floral and fruity aromas. It is very lacey on the palate, finishing with a lingering touch of welcome acidity. Good served with sautéed scallops.

• Jean-Paul Paquet, 71960 Fuissé, tel. 03.85.27.01.06, fax 03.85.27.01.07, e-mail fussiacus@wanadoo.fr   by appt.

□
DOM. DES GERBEAUX
Cuvée Prestige Très vieilles vignes 1999★

0.4 ha 2,800 €11-15

Béatrice and Jean-Michel Drouin, who preside brilliantly over the fortunes of this estate, are ardent supporters of the appellation. Faithful readers of the Guide will not be surprised to find three of their wines chosen again this year. This one is appealing with its light, pale-yellow colour and subtle aromas (spring flowers, hawthorn, dried fruits and toast) and its balance of wine and oak. It is a fresh, fruity wine that could be laid down for four to five years. Just as elegant is the **Terroir de Pouilly et Fuissé 2000**, still rather reserved at the moment but with fine potential, notably because of the richness on the palate. As to the **Terroir de Soluté 2000**, it is already manifesting, loud and clear, exotic notes of grapefruit and pineapple; slightly acidic and very fresh on the palate.

• Jean-Michel Drouin, Les Gerbeaux, 71960 Solutré-Pouilly, tel. 03.85.35.80.17, fax 03.85.35.87.12   by appt.

□
YVES GIROUX Cuvée Chêne 1999★

1 ha 3,500 €11-15

Very delicate with notes of linden blossom, honey and undergrowth, this intense gold-coloured wine is powerful, round and long on the palate; it needs to be laid down for several years. 'It could be drunk in a year's time or laid down for 15 years,' one taster concluded.

• Dom. Yves Giroux, Les Molards, 71960 Fuissé, tel. 03.85.35.63.64, fax 03.85.32.90.08   by appt.

□
DOM. JEAN GOYON 1999★

2 ha 5,000 €8-11

At the foot of the Solutré rock, Jean Goyon has created this delicate wine, product of 40-year-old vines, with the pronounced aroma of spring flowers that is characteristic of the Chardonnay grape grown in clay-limestone soil. It should be drunk now to appreciate its freshness.

• Jean Goyon, Au Bourg, 71960 Solutré-Pouilly, tel. 03.85.35.81.15, fax 03.85.35.87.03   by appt.

□
MME RENE GUERIN La Roche 2000

0.18 ha 1,200 €11-15

Intense gold-yellow in colour, this Pouilly-Fuissé, though dry, shows all the traits of overripe grapes. The powerful, fruity nose has crystallised fruit aromas. The attack is straightforward; on the palate it is round and full, enhanced by an attractive freshness resulting from its well-adjusted acidity. The flavours on the middle palate are exotic and honeyed. A wine to serve from now onwards, with foie gras.

• Mme René Guérin, Le Martelet, 71960 Vergisson, tel. 03.85.35.84.39   by appt.

□
LA CROIX-PARDON 1999★★

6 ha 40,000 €11-15

Erected in the 19th century to watch over the Pouilly-Fuissé appellation, La Croix-Pardon does indeed seem to have protected this wine. Draped in amber-gold, it is packed with powerful aromas where crystallised fruits, wax polish and honey all combine together. Round and full on the palate, it has buttery, honeyed flavours. 'A rich, full and satisfying wine,' was one taster's opinion.

• Joseph Burrier, Ch. de Beauregard, 71960 Fuissé, tel. 03.85.35.60.76, fax 03.85.35.66.04, e-mail joseph.burrier@magcos.com
• F.-M. Burrier

□
DOM. DE LALANDE
Clos Reyssié 1999★

n.c. 3,500 €11-15

Situated on the magnificent east-facing hillside in the village of Chaintré, the Clos

Pouilly-Fuissé

ANDRE AUVIGUE La Frairie 1999★★
n.c. 3,500 📦⃝ €11–15

This is a Pouilly-Fuissé with plenty of character. Maturation carried out partly in large wooden casks has enhanced the quality of the grapes, which came from good stock. It has aromas of spring flowers and lemon, typically Chardonnay, opening out with hints of toast. While still delicate on the palate, it is promising and well-balanced, with notes of peonies and overblown roses. An extremely well-made wine.

☎ André Auvigue, 71960 Solutré-Pouilly, tel. 03.85.35.80.80, fax 03.85.34.75.89 ▼
🍴 by appt.

CH. DE BEAUREGARD
La Maréchaude 1999★★★
1.2 ha 8,000 📦⃝ €15–23

Isolated on the wine-producing plateau of Fuissé, Château de Beauregard stands proudly facing the Solutré and Vergisson rocks. In charge since 1999, Frédéric-Marc Burrier knows how to get the best out of the fabulous Pouilly-Fuissé *terroirs* (19 ha/47 acres), notably by ploughing the soil. This year he won all the votes. This instantly appealing 99 has a brilliant green-gold colour with tremendous finesse in its aromas of violets, vanilla, butter and fruit (dried apricots). The same complexity is found on a palate that is rich, full, and toasty with mocha flavours. 'Impressively well-balanced and elegant on the palate,' one taster enthused. Ideal to drink with a *poularde de Bresse*. The **Pouilly-Fuissé 99 du Château** also impressed the Jury with its toasty, charred character; it was awarded one star.

☎ Joseph Burrier, Ch. de Beauregard, 71960 Fuissé, tel. 03.85.35.60.76, fax 03.85.35.66.04, e-mail joseph.burrier@mageos.com ▼ 🍴 by appt.

FRANCOIS BOURDON
Le Clos Cuvée réservée 1999
0.53 ha 1,000 ▪⃝ €8–11

At the head of this 13-ha (32-acre) estate since 1995, François Bourdon uses traditional methods of vinification, with a fairly

657

long fermentation period followed by maturation on lees for ten months. A sparkling yellow colour, this wine has an open, floral and fruity aroma. On the palate it is full and round with plenty of richness but retains a certain liveliness. It will be excellent with fish cooked in cream in one to two years' time.

☎ François Bourdon, Pouilly, 71960 Solutré-Pouilly, tel. 03.85.35.81.44, fax 03.85.35.81.44

DOM. MICHEL CHEVEAU 1999★
4 ha 1,500 📦⃝ ◆ €8–11

This family-owned domaine, situated in the centre of the hamlet of Pouilly, has 11 ha (27.2 acres) of vineyards. Nowadays, Nicholas, 23, produces the wine and, as far as one can tell, he has made an excellent start with these two well-executed wines. The **Vieilles Vignes 99** may be mentioned for its toasty and vanilla aromas, but it is still not very forthcoming. The little goats' cheeses that they make here in the Mâcon area are greatly looking forward to it.

☎ Dom. Michel Cheveau, Pouilly, 71960 Solutré-Pouilly, tel. 03.85.35.81.50, fax 03.85.35.87.88 ▼ 🍴 by appt.

DOM. CORDIER PERE ET FILS
Vers Cras 1999★★
0.3 ha 2,000 📦⃝ €23–30

The Cordier estate is today one of the leading domaines in the Mâcon area. It submitted several attractive wines: the **Vers Pouilly 99** and the **Les Vignes Blanches 99** are commended for their fullness and structure, but still need time for the oak to integrate. On the other hand, this Vers Cras came out the winner with a unanimous *coup de cœur*. After 15 months in oak, its colour is a brilliant yellow-gold. The aroma opens on nutty notes (hazelnuts, praline) and toast. The exceptional roundness on the palate makes it extremely attractive, and the fullness of its flavours of orange peel, bergamot and honey all go to mark it out as one of the appellation's nobility.

☎ Dom. Cordier Père et Fils, 71960 Fuissé, tel. 03.85.35.62.89, fax 03.85.35.64.01
🍴 by appt.

PIERRE DUPOND 2000
n.c. n.c. ▪⃝ €11–15

A *négoce* specialising in Beaujolais wines, Pierre Dupond here presented this Pouilly-Fuissé which caught the Jury's attention. The appealing quality of this 2000 vintage with

BURGUNDY